my mindful day

Empathy

Published in the United States of America by Cherry Lake Publishing
Ann Arbor, Michigan
www.cherrylakepublishing.com

Reading Adviser: Marla Conn, MS, Ed., Literacy specialist, Read-Ability, Inc.
Book Designer: Jennifer Wahi
Illustrator: Jeff Bane

Photo Credits: ©Lordn/Shutterstock, 5; ©Rawpixel.com/Shutterstock, 7, 15; ©Pixel-Shot/Shutterstock, 9; ©Zdravinjo/Shutterstock, 11; ©Africa Studio/Shutterstock, 13; ©Monkey Business Images/Shutterstock, 17, 23; ©YAKOBCHUK VIACHESLAV/Shutterstock, 19; ©pixfly/Shutterstock, 21; Cover, 6, 8, 18, Jeff Bane; Various vector images throughout courtesy of Shutterstock.com

Library of Congress Cataloging-in-Publication Data has been filed and is available at catalog.loc.gov

Printed in the United States of America

table of contents

About the author: Katie Marsico is the author of more than 200 reference books for children and young adults. She lives with her husband and six children near Chicago, Illinois.

About the illustrator: Jeff Bane and his two business partners own a studio along the American River in Folsom, California, home of the 1849 Gold Rush. When Jeff's not sketching or illustrating for clients, he's either swimming or kayaking in the river to relax.

"How would *you* feel?"

We ask this question for a reason.

It builds **empathy**.

More than our own feelings matter.

The world is filled with people.

We need to be **mindful** of them.

Love and friendship help make us happy.

Yet we don't always think of others' feelings.

How do you feel if people don't listen?

Angry or sad?

Other people feel the same.

This often leads to **conflict**.

During conflict, our **focus** is on fighting.

Stress makes our mind race.

We rush past our own feelings.

When do you feel stressed?

Empathy is best for everyone.

But building it takes work.

First, we must grow more mindful.

Our lives are busy.

We must pause and listen.

That's how we learn about others' feelings.

What else can you learn by listening?

It helps to talk in person.

Texts don't always show feelings.

Sometimes computers and phones **distract** us.

Our mind should be clear.

We're more aware when we focus.

That's why some people **meditate**.

It's also why some do **yoga**.

Other people shape our world.

We shape theirs too.

Our feelings form shared stories.

Empathy makes us kinder!

How can you be mindful today?

glossary & index

glossary

conflict (KAHN-flikt) a fight or struggle

distract (dih-STRAKT) to direct your attention away from something else

empathy (EM-puh-thee) understanding how another person feels

focus (FOH-kuhs) to give your attention to

meditate (MED-ih-tate) to train your mind to relax and focus

mindful (MINDE-ful) aware of your body, mind, and feelings

yoga (YOH-guh) poses, breathing, and sometimes meditation and chanting that provide balance and good health

index